God's power in you is trusting in our father at all times. keeping your eyes on Him!

By: Sylvia Burris

Published by Open Heaven Ministry Oakboro, NC 28129

A heartfelt appreciation to Andrew Wommack Ministry and CMM College of Theology in Charlotte for providing me with resources and education. Blessings to you all.

God's Power through you!

For Nathan Huneycutt,

My books are a tribute to the man who never stopped praying for my return home. I want everyone to understand the strength of prayer, knowing that you will also witness your lost child or grandchild coming back. He loved me unconditionally and always spoke truth into my life. Similarly, by being honest and caring with your children and grandchildren, they will one day benefit from the values you instilled, just as I did. Thank you, grandpa, for never giving up on me, your prodigal, as I finally found my way back home.

Elaine and Johnny Thomas,

To my friends who never gave up on me, guided me, and offered help along the way, you are truly a blessing. I wouldn't have reached where I am today without your support. Thank you.

Yes, Jesus went through all of Galilee, teaching in the synagogues, preaching the gospel, and healing all manner of sickness and diseases among the people. In this same way, Jesus does the same today for everyone who believes in His word and receives healing through faith.   Matthew 4:23

Father, I accept your healing in my body at this moment in the name of Jesus! Thank you, Jesus!

The Word of God is the will of God, and it shows us that it's always God's will to heal. When Jesus was confronted by the leper if he would heal him. "I will!" Jesus replied. In all cases of healing, Jesus never turned anyone down or made them wait.

Is sickness our punishment?

Some churches today will say God is "Sovereign" meaning that he controls everything, but that's not true. The word "sovereign," is not used in the King James. It is used in the Old Testament; only is used for "LORD". According to Peter, "The Lord does not wish for any to perish, but for all to come to repentance." Because of God's freedom, we are choosing to perish. Just as Jesus took the punishment for our sins, he took the punishment for our sicknesses too. Our freedom and healing is based soley on what Jesus did on the cross. Our faith activates that salvation and healing.

"The 'thorn' mentioned in Paul's revelations wasn't an illness, but a messenger sent to prevent him from being exalted by God in the eyes of the public. This persecution aimed to scare the weak-hearted from dedicating their lives to God. In his writing, Paul recounts experiences like shipwrecks, beatings, and being left for dead, as well as imprisonment, none of which indicate sickness but rather the challenges he faced. The term 'messenger' refers to a created being, suggesting that his 'thorn' was essentially a demon sent to trouble him. It was persecution, not an illness."

What does Jesus want us to do for our healing?

Similar to the man with the withered hand who reached out to Jesus when He told him to stretch out his hand, we are encouraged to take a step of faith and do what seems impossible. Just as Jesus instructed Mary at Lazarus's tomb to believe and witness the glory of God, the key lies in believing, speaking, and acting in faith to experience God's glory in our circumstances.

Matthew 3:1-6, John 11:40

When you give a gift to someone, there's no need to ask for it back, and similarly, with Jesus. He sacrificed himself on the cross to secure your salvation and healing. Just accept it, like a friend receiving a gift from you. In the story of the blind men seeking sight from Jesus, they believed in His ability. Jesus responded, "According to your faith, let it be done," and healed them by touching their eyes.

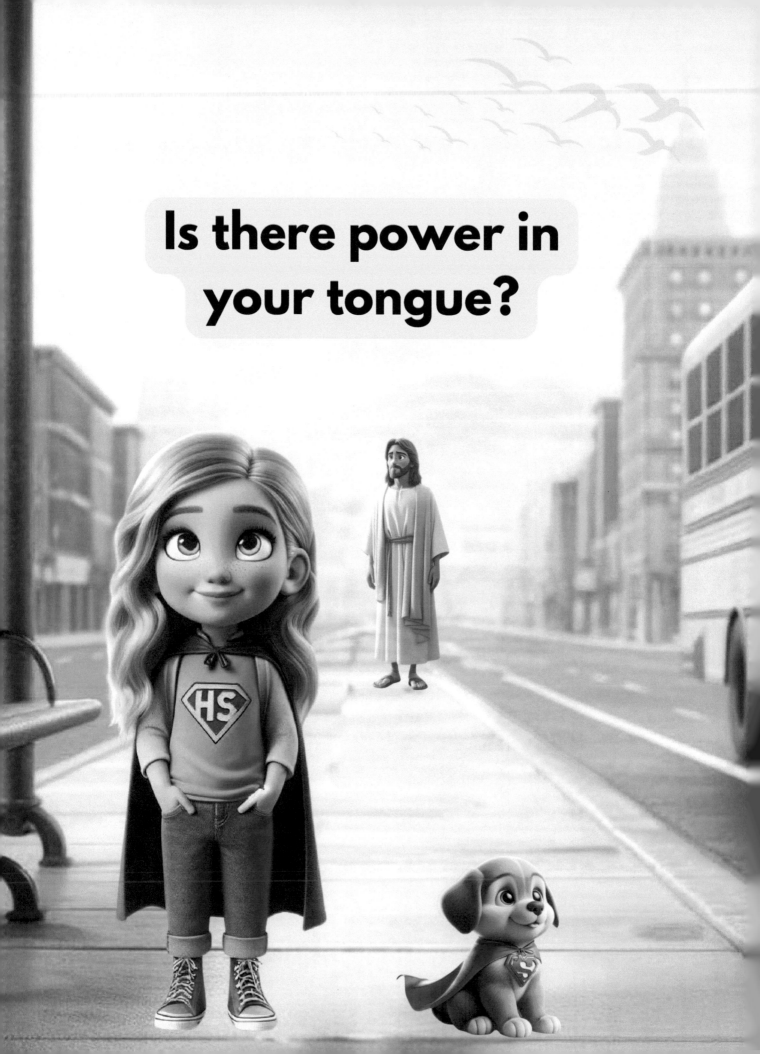

Life and death lie in the power of speech. Our words have the ability to either bless or curse us. It's important to be mindful because speaking negatively about being sick can actually manifest illness. Our words act as seeds, determining what we will reap. Therefore, speak life and positivity over your circumstances, and witness the transformation that follows.

Proverbs 18:21

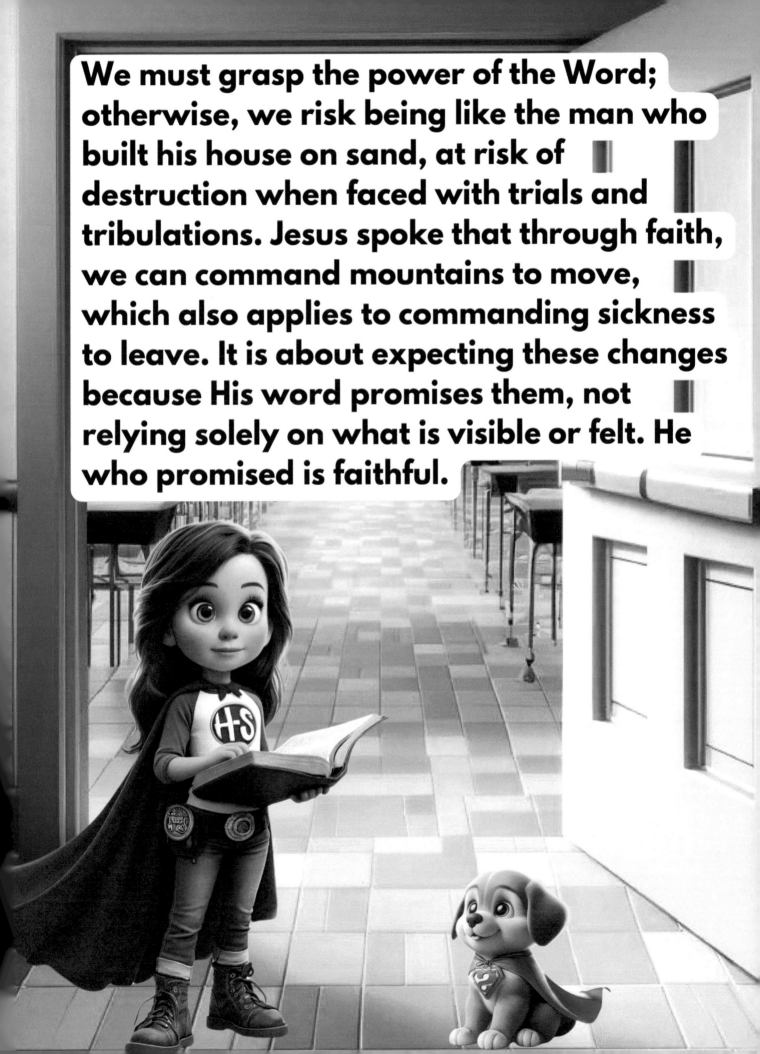

We must grasp the power of the Word; otherwise, we risk being like the man who built his house on sand, at risk of destruction when faced with trials and tribulations. Jesus spoke that through faith, we can command mountains to move, which also applies to commanding sickness to leave. It is about expecting these changes because His word promises them, not relying solely on what is visible or felt. He who promised is faithful.

While praying for a friend with an open wound on her side, I asked if she had forgiven her ex-husband. She responded with a firm "no." I explained that forgiveness is essential for healing, and we prayed together. After forgiving him, she shared that the wound had healed the following morning. The Bible says, "forgive so that we can be forgiven by God."

Doubt significantly impacts the healing process. When Jesus visited his hometown, he couldn't heal many due to their lack of belief. Some doubt that He continues to heal today, but Jesus remains constant – unchanged yesterday, today, and forever. While some believe sickness is a lesson from God, he does not inflict sickness any more than he does sins. Jesus emphasized, "Just believe, and you will witness God's glory."

Meet Sylvia

Sylvia Burris leads Open Heaven Ministry as the main pastor. Her mission is to educate children about their authority in Christ and empower them to experience miracles, signs, and wonders with the guidance of the Holy Spirit. Sylvia, a mother of three, is nurturing her children who are actively involved in the healing ministry. Her ultimate goal is to spread the love of God across the globe.

Keeping your focus on God, remember that all things are possible with Him. Regardless of your age, God has empowered you to overcome the enemy's actions. So, rise up like a Superhero and pray for those who are sick. With the Holy Spirit's strength and power within you, you will witness people being healed in the name of Jesus. Thank you for exploring this book on common questions about healing. Remember, God loves you, and so do I.